LITTLE MISS TV
AT THE SEASID

Little Miss Twins are at the seaside. Little Miss Twin and Little Miss Twin both want an ice-cream. Can you show them the way?

MR CLEVER'S FALLING OVER DANCE

Mr Clever dreams he's in France,
Where Mr Clever thinks he can dance!
Mr Clever stands on his head!
But, oh dear!
Mr Clever falls out of bed!

MR SILLY GETS WET!

Mr Silly went to sea
In a boat that looked like a giant pea.
He bobbed about on the crest of a wave.
He nearly got wet,
What a close shave!
But then, when he stepped back on dry land,
He stumbled and slipped and slid on the sand...
SPLASH!

6

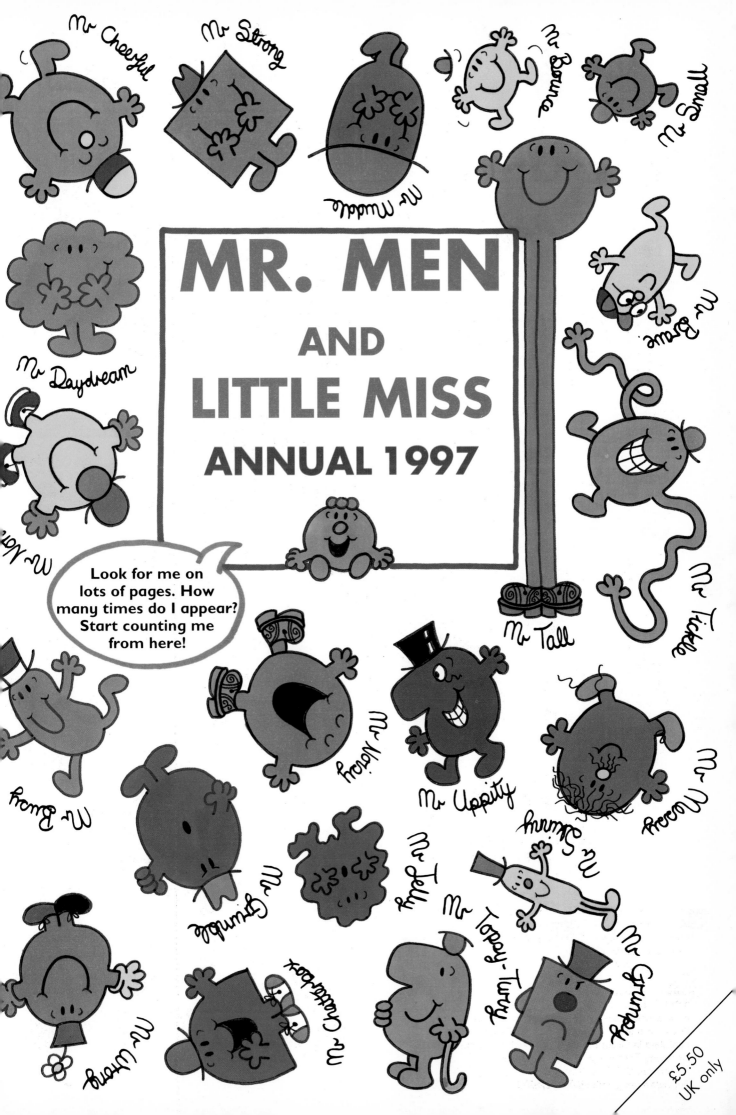

Mr Happy

1 "I feel so very happy," sang Mr Happy, doing a little dance. "I think I'll ask Mr Snow to come round for tea." Which is exactly what he did.

2 But it was sunny and hot as they sat in the garden. "Oh no!" said Mr Snow. "I think I'm starting to melt." Mr Happy looked worried.

3 "I know, we'll have our tea somewhere else," he said. So Mr Happy packed everything up and put it into his car. And off they went.

4 "I think you'll feel much better very soon," said Mr Happy. But Mr Snow wasn't so sure. "Only if we get out of this hot sun!" he said.

5 They stopped outside a building. Mr Snow looked puzzled. "Where are we?" he asked. "Bring the tea things," said Mr Happy.

6 It was an ice rink. Mr Happy and Mr Snow had their tea on the ice. Mr Snow stopped melting. "Oooh, I like it here," he said.

LITTLE MISS SPLENDID'S
SPLENDID BANANA MILKSHAKE

You will need...
1 banana
1/4 litre of milk
1 teaspoon of honey
a fork, mixing bowl,
spoon and glass

Try my yummy drink.
It's easy to make and
tastes absolutely
splendid!

1 Peel the banana,
then mash it in a bowl
with a fork.

3 Carefully pour the milk in,
stirring with a fork.

4 Pour the milkshake into
a glass – and enjoy it!

2 Mix in the
honey with a spoon.

7

THE GREAT EGG RACE

Sometimes has a very good idea. Sometimes Mr Messy's

ideas are very, very messy. Let me tell you about his messiest idea of

all. He sent  to 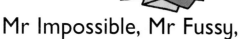 5 of his friends. He wrote to 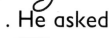 ,

Mr Impossible, Mr Fussy,  and  . He asked

them to his for a race. Not a running race. Not a

race, not even a hop-along race.  asked them to

each bring a  . They were going to have an and

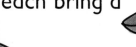 race. He would bring the 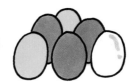 , 6 of them.

Can you guess what happened? I said it was a messy idea, didn't I?

Well, first of all,  said he wasn't going to play. He said

it was impossible to race without his falling off his 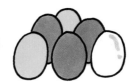 .

Then said he didn't like the white egg  had

given him. He wanted a egg instead. Poor Mr Messy! He told

that it wasn't impossible to race with an [egg] on his spoon. Then he swapped [Mr Happy]'s brown [egg] for Mr Fussy's white [egg]. Everyone was ready. The Great Egg Race could begin.

Well, almost. [Mr Snow] said he wanted to race with a [snowball] on his [spoon]. "But it won't be an [egg] race then!" said Mr Messy. Now they were ready. Or were they? "Where's [Mr Lazy]?" said [Mr Bounce]. "We can't start without him!" "Look! He's fast asleep under that big [tree]," said [Mr Funny]. "Then let's race over to him," said Mr Messy. "The winner is the one who gets there without breaking their [egg]!" On the count of [3] they were off. One by one the eggs slipped off their [spoon] and smashed on the ground.

When they reached Mr Lazy there were no [eggs] left – except for [Mr Lazy]'s white one. "How cunning!" said Mr Messy. "You missed the race, but you still have your [egg]. You are the winner!"

Little Miss Trouble

1 "Shall I be really good today?" said Little Miss Trouble. "Or shall I be naughty? I just can't decide what to do. What a peculiar day it seems to be!"

2 Now this wasn't like her at all, was it? You know what Little Miss Trouble likes to do best. Look what she did to Little Miss Neat's shopping!

3 And don't forget what she did to Mr Messy's garden. He'd never seen anything like it! It looked awful. He had to untidy it all over again – fast!

4 Then there was the day she told Little Miss Brainy that two plus two made five. Oh, dear! All that counting gave Little Miss Brainy a headache!

5 What about the trick she played on Mr Slow? Putting oil on the path certainly made him walk a lot faster – but he wasn't very pleased!

6 So back to today. "I think this is a 'trouble free day'," she said. "A day for thinking up new tricks. It's going to be a good day after all!"

MR FUNNY
AND THE MIXED-UP CLOTHES

"Hello, I'm Mr Funny. I've just played a joke on my Mr Men friends!
While they were in the swimming pool I mixed up all their clothes!"
Can you help the Mr Men find their hats and shoes?

Mr Silly   Mr Uppity   Mr Strong   Mr Nonsense   Mr Dizzy   Mr Clever

Answers on page 63

MR BUSY
AND HIS PICTURE PRESENTS

"Hello, I'm Mr Busy. Here are two pictures I drew to give to the Little Miss Twins. They are supposed to be the same but I was too busy to copy them properly. There are five things different in the bottom picture. Can you tell me what they are?"

12

Answers on page 63

LITTLE MISS CURIOUS
AND THE MIXED-UP SHADOWS

"Hello, I'm Little Miss Curious. Have you ever wondered where shadows come from? I have. If you draw lines to match the shadow shapes to their owners, you'll soon find out where these shadows have come from!"

Answers on page 63

WHO ATE ALL THE CAKES?

On Saturday,  went to the shop. But first, he had

his usual big breakfast – three , four slices of  (with

lots of) and five  of tea. Then he looked for his biggest

bag and set off to the . In the distance he saw

 and she had a HUGE 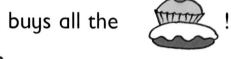 with her! "Oh, no!" he

said. "I must hurry, before Little Miss Greedy buys all the !"

So he started to run all the way to the  shop. But, oh, no, the

 was closed! There was a little notice in the . It said:

"Sold Out". Poor ! A day without any cakes. So what

do you think he did? He went to 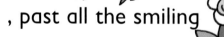 roly poly .

He walked along her , past all the smiling , past all

the 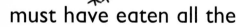 eating crumbs…What? Crumbs? Oh, no! Little Miss Greedy

must have eaten all the  and given the crumbs to the !

So, 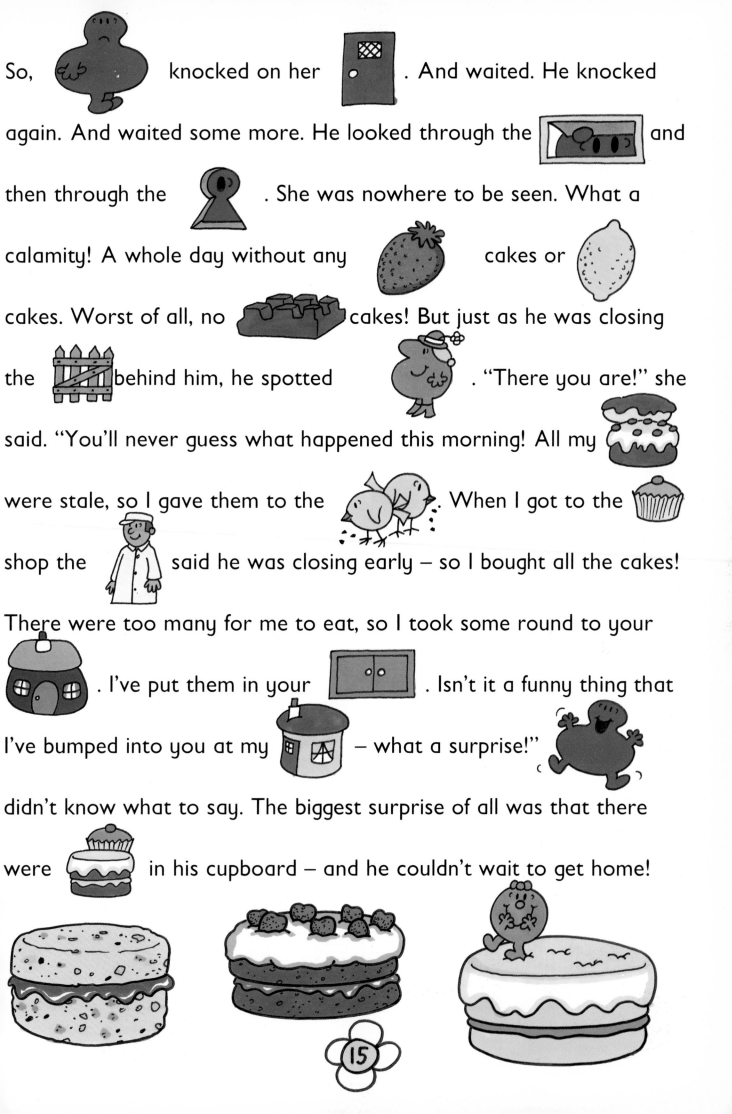 knocked on her ▨ . And waited. He knocked again. And waited some more. He looked through the ▤ and then through the ▲ . She was nowhere to be seen. What a calamity! A whole day without any 🍓 cakes or 🍋 cakes. Worst of all, no ▦ cakes! But just as he was closing the ▨ behind him, he spotted 👒 . "There you are!" she said. "You'll never guess what happened this morning! All my 🍰 were stale, so I gave them to the 🐦 . When I got to the 🧁 shop the 👨‍🍳 said he was closing early – so I bought all the cakes! There were too many for me to eat, so I took some round to your 🏠 . I've put them in your 🚪 . Isn't it a funny thing that I've bumped into you at my 🏠 – what a surprise!"

didn't know what to say. The biggest surprise of all was that there were 🎂 in his cupboard – and he couldn't wait to get home!

15

Mr Nosey

1 When Mr Nosey looked over his fence, being nosey, of course, he saw Mr Quiet's new shed. "I wonder what's inside," he said.

2 So he climbed over the fence and opened the shed door. What a surprise! Out flew lots of chickens. "Oh, what have I done?" he said.

3 The chickens made so much noise that Mr Quiet came to see what was going on. "Ssshh! Please bring them all back!" he said.

4 So Mr Nosey chased them all around the garden, up and down the trees, and in and out of the house. "This is hard work!" he said.

5 The chickens liked the garden and had a great time jumping over Mr Nosey. They thought it was a game. Mr Nosey didn't!

6 When it got dark, the chickens landed on Mr Nosey's nose. "Time for bed," they said. "I wish I wasn't so nosey!" said Mr Nosey.

LITTLE MISS STAR'S
CHOCOLATE CRISPY CAKES

Try my delicious chocolate crispy cakes – they're so easy to make!

You will need...
50g chocolate
25g rice crispies
a handful of raisins
a medium-sized mixing bowl
a spoon
paper cake cases

1 Melt the chocolate.
Ask a grown-up to do this for you. Tell them to break the chocolate into pieces and put it into a bowl over hot water. (Or they could use a microwave oven.)

2 When the chocolate is runny, pour in the rice crispies and raisins.

3 Stir with a spoon until all the rice crispies and raisins are covered with chocolate.

4 Spoon into paper cake cases and put them in the fridge to set.

5 Leave for about 15 minutes, then they're ready to eat!

LITTLE MISS DOTTY'S BAND

Roll up! Roll up! It's come to town!
The Little Miss Dotty Band!
Just come and listen to it folks!
The worst band in the land!

An elephant plays the trumpet!
The harpist is a squid!
An ostrich plays the tuba!
On piano is a pig!

An octopus is the drummer!
On banjo is a snail!
A chimp is on the cello!
And the singer is a whale!

A centipede does a tap dance!
On flute a unicorn!
A monkey plays the bongos!
And the rhino plays his horn!

Roll up! Roll up! It's come to town!
The Little Miss Dotty Band!
And, guess what she has called it?
It's called The Elastic Band!

18

MR STRONG'S
WORD PUZZLE

"Mr Men and Little Misses are very colourful," says Mr Strong. "I'm red, Mr Happy is yellow and Little Miss Brainy is blue. Can you find the names of colours hidden in my puzzle? There are eight to find. Draw lines through them when you find each word."

G	F	R	E	D	P	O	L
B	L	U	E	B	U	A	P
R	E	N	E	E	R	G	I
O	L	O	T	I	P	E	N
W	M	J	B	L	L	T	K
N	M	I	Z	C	E	I	B
N	K	O	L	L	E	H	K
W	O	L	L	E	Y	W	R

Tick them off as you find the hidden colours:

red ☐   green ☐   brown ☐   purple ☐
blue ☐   yellow ☐   white ☐   pink ☐

19

 # THE LOST HANDBAG

Little Miss Somersault likes to keep fit. In fact, she is the fittest person I know.

As soon as she wakes up she does three high jumps in the air, followed by four handstands, and then head over heels, five times.

Now, a few days ago, this is what happened next.

"Today feels like a day for lots of exercise," she said, bending down to touch her toes, six times.

And that was when Little Miss Contrary came running along, out of breath. "Hello," she said, in a panting sort of a voice. "Have you dropped something?"

"Don't be silly!" said Little Miss Somersault. "I'm touching my toes because I'm exercising!"

"Does that mean you're also good at running?" asked Little Miss Contrary. "Because if it does, you might be able to help me."

Little Miss Contrary explained that Little Miss Scatterbrain had been to visit her, but had left her handbag behind. "You could run after her. You'll catch her up before I do," she said.

Little Miss Somersault took the handbag and set off to Buttercup Cottage, which was where Little Miss Scatterbrain lived.

Now, if you or I had run that far, it would have taken three and a half minutes. But for Little Miss Somersault it took no time at all.

20

She knocked on the door. No reply. So she sat down and waited. But you know what Little Miss Somersault is like. She can't sit still for long. She started exercising. Three headstands, four press-ups then five laps of the garden.

"But," began Little Miss Somersault, "this is your handbag. You left it at Little Miss Contrary's house."

"Oh, did I?" said Little Miss Scatterbrain, in a sheepish sort of a voice. "Wherever I go I leave my handbag behind – and then end up buying another one exactly the same! Then someone brings my old handbag back to me. So now I've got thirty identical handbags, not to mention the forty identical hats, the fifty identical pairs of gloves or the—"

"Coo-ee," called a voice. It was Little Miss Scatterbrain. "Here I am. Oh, what a lovely handbag you've got," she said, pointing at the handbag Little Miss Somersault was holding. "I've just bought one exactly the same as yours."

Little Miss Somersault didn't wait to hear the rest of the list. "Sorry, can't stay any longer," she said. "I promised I'd show Little Miss Contrary how to do cartwheels. Bye bye!" And off she went, cartwheeling all the way back to her house.

Little Miss Bossy

1 It was quiet in the library. But then, it was meant to be quiet. The library was the quietest place Little Miss Helpful knew, and she liked it.

2 Now one day, a few days before yesterday, there was an…er…well, see for yourself. That's what happened when Little Miss Bossy arrived.

3 "Ssshhh," said Little Miss Helpful. "Keep the noise down." "Speak up!" said Little Miss Bossy. "I can't," said Little Miss Helpful. "Sssshhh!"

4 "Who are you telling to 'sssshhh'?" asked Little Miss Bossy. "All I'm trying to do is find a book!" "Let me help you then," said Little Miss Helpful.

5 "What book are you looking for? One on weight lifting? Or jam-making? Or could it be one on good manners?" said Little Miss Helpful.

6 "Hmmpphh!" huffed Little Miss Bossy. "I don't need your help!" And she left. "That's better," said Little Miss Helpful. "I'm glad I helped!"

MR SLOW
AND HIS NOT VERY FAST MAZE

Mr Slow never does anything fast. He does everything in his own time, slowly, just when it suits him. Take this maze, for instance. You or I would race through it in no time. But Mr Slow, well, he needs a little help. Can you show him the way through?

MR RUSH
AND OTHER THINGS IN A HURRY

"Sorry, can't stop for long. Got to go here there and everywhere, and I'm terribly late. I'll have to rush! Oh, almost forgot to say, I'm not the only one in a hurry – look who else has been rushed off their feet, wings and wheels! Bye!"

The Cheetah is the fastest animal on land. It can run at up to 60 miles an hour.

I'm going as fast as I can but I can't keep up with this bicycle! One rider once went at more than 150 miles an hour on his bike. He must have been in a bigger rush than me!

The fastest bird is the Peregrine Falcon. When it swoops down out of the sky it can reach a speed of 150 miles an hour.

Some spiders can run at up to 10 miles an hour. I'd be running at 11 miles an hour, just to stay in front of them!

24

 # Mr Greedy

1 It was Mr Greedy's birthday and he made himself a huge birthday breakfast with six eggs, ten slices of toast with jam and seven cups of tea!

2 Later he went for a walk and met Mr Bump and Mr Tickle. "Happy birthday, Mr Greedy!" they said and gave him a big birthday cake with candles on.

3 Then Mr Happy came along with a present. It was a big basket of rosy red apples. Mr Greedy was delighted! He liked apples very much!

4 "Happy birthday!" Mr Strong and Mr Jelly said together. Mr Strong gave him a plate of cakes and Mr Jelly gave him a huge, wobbly tray of jellies.

5 Mr Greedy had lots of presents now. "How can I carry all these presents home safely without dropping anything?" he thought.

6 He had a good idea. Mr Greedy ate up all his presents! "Now I'm carrying them all in my tum!" he said, patting his HUGE tummy!

DANDELION COUNTING

Little Miss Fickle lived in Dandelion Cottage. She had wanted to call it Rose Cottage, but then she had changed her mind. She thought Tulip Cottage might sound better. But then she had changed her mind again and decided to call it Chrysanthemum Cottage.

Now she liked the sound of that most of all. But by the time she had learned to say it properly, her garden had grown full of dandelions. There wasn't a rose, tulip or a chrysanthemum in sight. So she called her house Dandelion Cottage instead.

One day she was counting all her dandelions, when along came Little Miss Stubborn.

"Coo-ee, Little Miss Stubborn," called out Little Miss Fickle. "Come over here, please."

"No!" said Little Miss Stubborn.

"Well, I'll come over to you then," said Little Miss Fickle. Which is just what she did. "I'd like to ask you a favour," she said to Little Miss Stubborn.

"I've been counting all my dandelions, and I can't decide if I've got two hundred and five, or five hundred and two. "I was wondering if you'd count them with me."

"Oh, I'm far too busy for that," said Little Miss Stubborn. "Far too busy indeed."

Just at that moment along came Little Miss Greedy. "Hello," she said. "My, your garden looks lovely with all those dandelions," she said to Little Miss Fickle.

"Does it?" asked Little Miss Fickle. "Is it really lovely?"

"It's the loveliest dandelion garden I know," said Little Miss Greedy. "It's so lovely, I could spend all day looking at it."

"Well," began Little Miss Fickle, "if you think it's that nice, maybe you'd like to help me find out how many dandelions I've got."

"Er…" began Little Miss Greedy.

"And if you're very lucky you might find the big chocolate cake that I've hidden in the garden," said Little Miss Fickle.

"I'll start right away!" said Little Miss Greedy. So off she ran.

"Did you say chocolate cake?" asked Little Miss Stubborn, quietly. "Well, maybe I could help you count your dandelions, after all," she said.

But, oh, dear! What a sight they saw when they got into Little Miss Fickle's garden. Little Miss Greedy was trampling all over the dandelions looking for the chocolate cake.

"I've looked everywhere," said Little Miss Greedy. "There's no chocolate cake here."

"Oh, well, I must have changed my mind and left it somewhere else," said Little Miss Fickle.

That was the worst thing she could have said, wasn't it? Off ran Little Miss Greedy, quickly followed by Little Miss Stubborn.

"Hey, come back," called out Little Miss Fickle. "You haven't counted my dandelions yet!" she shouted after them.

But you can count them for her, can't you?

27

Mr Tickle

1 Mr Tickle watched the postman walking along with his sack of letters. He couldn't resist reaching out with his long arms and tickling him!

2 The postman jumped and the letters flew out of his sack. They landed in a muddle on the ground. "Look what you've done," he said. He was cross!

3 PC Blue came by. "I saw that. It was very naughty, Mr Tickle," he said. Mr Tickle looked at the pile of letters on the ground. He was very sorry.

4 "I'll put things right," he said. He picked up all the letters. Then with his l-o-n-g arm he delivered a letter past a very playful dog!

5 Then Mr Tickle delivered the letters to all the people in the flats. The postman was very pleased – he didn't have to climb the stairs!

LITTLE MISS BUSY'S
WORD PUZZLE

At night, Little Miss Busy has busy dreams, writing out shopping lists.
Here's the list she wrote last night. You'll see eight words at the
bottom of the page. Can you find them hidden in her puzzle?
Look forwards and backwards, and up and down.
Draw lines through them when you find each word.

G	J	R	E	D	P	P	L
B	A	N	A	N	A	O	P
R	M	N	E	E	R	T	I
E	L	O	S	U	G	A	R
A	M	J	E	L	L	T	K
D	M	T	E	A	E	O	B
N	K	O	H	L	E	H	K
W	O	L	C	R	E	A	M

Tick them off as you find the hidden words:

jam	☐	cheese	☐	sugar	☐	bread	☐
tea	☐	potato	☐	cream	☐	banana	☐

29

SSSHH! QUIET PLEASE!

Mr Chatterbox was talking to Mr Grumble. He was doing enough talking for both of them. Each time Mr Grumble tried to say something, Mr Chatterbox thought of something else to say.

"Ah-hem!" said Mr Grumble.

"And as I was saying," continued Mr Chatterbox.

Which, of course, they were not. That was just Mr Mischief playing a joke on Mr Chatterbox, and also on Mr Grumble.

"Bah!" said Mr Grumble. "It was my turn to speak! Now Mr Chatterbox has started talking again. Just listen to him!"

"Bah!" said Mr Grumble. Just then, Mr Mischief came along. "Hello," he said. "Lovely day for a chat."

"Bah!" said Mr Grumble. "It might be a lovely day to you, but I've been waiting for ages to say something to Mr Chatterbox!"

At which point, Mr Chatterbox stopped just long enough for Mr Mischief to tell him that his shoelaces were undone.

"Well," said Mr Chatterbox, "if my shoelaces really were undone, it would have been good of you to tell me. Even though they were still tied up tightly, it was worth me checking them, just in case they really were coming loose…"

"Bah!" said Mr Grumble, again.

"If I were you," said Mr Mischief, whispering in Mr Grumble's ear, "I'd tell him that today is 'National No Chatting Day'. That might make him stop talking. Then you can say what you want to."

Mr Chatterbox slowly closed his mouth and swallowed the unfinished word. "Gulp!" he said.

"See, I told you it would work," said Mr Mischief, grinning.

"Ssshh!" said Mr Chatterbox to Mr Mischief. "Quiet please! Don't you know you shouldn't be talking today?"

"That'll never work. Not in a month of Sundays," he said, in a grumbling sort of a voice.

"Oh, well," said Mr Mischief. "You'll never find out unless you try, will you?"

Mr Grumble cleared his throat.

"Ah-hem!" he said, loudly, followed by "Bah!"

At which point Mr Chatterbox stopped talking, right in the middle of a word. Very quickly, Mr Grumble explained that today was 'National No Chatting Day', just like Mr Mischief had said.

And with that he was off again, explaining to Mr Grumble all about 'National No Chatting Day'. "I think it's a very good idea for everyone to be quiet today," he said. "I must go and tell as many people as I can!"

"So much for your good idea!" said Mr Grumble to Mr Mischief.

"Tricked you!" said Mr Mischief. But do you know something? Mr Grumble had the last word after all. "BAH!" he said.

What else could it have been?

MR SMALL
AND HIS TIN OF BEANS

One baked bean on a plate!
That's everything Mr Small eats!
And a can of baked beans,
When eaten like that,
Can last for
fifty-two weeks!

MR NOISY
PLAYS THE DRUMS!

Oh, dear! Oh, dear!
What's this I hear?
Mr Noisy's playing the drums!
But, what is worse,
Much worse, I fear!
Is, while he drums,
He **hums!**

32

LITTLE MISS BRAINY
AND THE SILLY SHAPES

'Hello, I'm Little Miss Brainy. I'm very good at most things. Well, at all things, actually. Especially at matching things. Like these silly shapes. Can you draw lines to match the shapes? Join the ones that are the same.'

33

Little Miss Naughty

1 What's the naughtiest thing you can think of? Running off with Mr Bump's bandages, like Little Miss Naughty did? Mr Bump got goosebumps!

2 Or swapping Little Miss Splendid's red hat with Little Miss Scatterbrain's green hat? Little Miss Naughty laughed so much she couldn't stand up!

3 Let me tell you what Little Miss Naughty did. She changed the numbers on people's houses. Number one became number two, and so on.

4 Now that was very, very naughty. Mr Tall thought Mr Small's house was his! And the postman took the wrong letters to every house!

5 But then Little Miss Naughty decided enough was enough. It was time to be good. It was time to put things back the right way again.

6 But she couldn't remember what was right and what was wrong. "What a mess!" she said. "It must be so much easier being good!"

MR PERFECT'S
PERFECT PACKET OF PEAS

"Hello, I'm Mr Perfect. Can you help me? I'm counting out pea seeds from a packet to plant in my garden. I'm putting them in groups of five. Would you draw more seeds so that each group has five? Thank you."

THE BROKEN VASE

Mr Dizzy had decided to help Mr Clumsy hang a picture on the wall. But he managed to hang it upside-down. Then Mr Clumsy slipped and pulled it down. He wouldn't have minded, except that it got caught in the curtains and pulled them down too, quickly followed by the curtain pole which just happened to knock a vase of flowers over.

"Phew!" said Mr Clumsy. "It could have been worse. At least the vase didn't break!"

At which point Mr Dizzy picked it up...slipped on the spilled water, fell over and dropped the vase. It broke into pieces.

"Ooops!" said Mr Dizzy. "Sorry."

They picked up the pieces of broken vase, all sixty-six of them, and put them into a bag.

"If we buy some glue, we can stick the vase together again," said Mr Dizzy.

On the way to the shops they met Mr Wrong. They told him about the broken vase.

"You don't want to use glue," he said. "It'll make a terrible mess. If I were you, I would use toothpaste."

Mr Dizzy and Mr Clumsy looked at each other in a funny sort of a way. But before they could say anything, Mr Wrong had tipped the bag upside-down. The sixty-six pieces of broken vase fell on to the ground, and smashed into even more pieces. Eighty-eight, to be precise.

"Steady on!" said Mr Clumsy.

"Be careful!" said Mr Dizzy.

"Pardon?" said Mr Wrong, turning even redder than he usually was, and pretending not to hear. In no time at all he'd squeezed toothpaste all over the pieces of broken vase.

"You're making a terrible mess," said Mr Clumsy.

"I don't think the pieces are sticking together at all," said Mr Dizzy.

pieces of broken vase up, put them back in the bag, and carried on walking.

"Just a moment," called out Mr Wrong. "I could use runny honey instead…or sticky toffee… or even gooey marmalade."

But Mr Dizzy and Mr Clumsy didn't think those were very good ideas. "No thank you," they said.

Do you know what they really used to stick the vase back together?

"Maybe if I used cheese spread instead of toothpaste," said Mr Wrong.

"No thank you!" said Mr Dizzy. "I think I'll stick to glue."

"Very funny!" said Mr Clumsy.

"Pardon?" said Mr Wrong, not sure what was funny at all.

They picked the eighty-eight

Well, I can tell you that it wasn't glue. Oh, no, not glue. They used sticky tape. Yards and yards and yards of it.

"Now, why didn't Mr Wrong think of that?" asked Mr Clumsy.

"Why indeed?" said Mr Dizzy. Well, what would you have used? Go on, tell me!

LITTLE MISS FUN'S
PAGE OF JOKES AND RIDDLES

MR TOPSY-TURVY'S
FUNNY FACE PIZZAS

Ooops! Why is my recipe page upside down?
It's all topsy-turvy – just like me!

You will need...
4 slices of French bread
tomato puree
cheese spread
tomato slices
pepper slices
olives
a plate and a knife

1 Spread the cheese on the bread.

2 Spread a thin layer of tomato puree on top of the cheese.

3 Make a funny face on each slice with the tomatoes, peppers and olives.

Make a smiley face with olive eyes, a tomato nose and a slice of pepper for a mouth.

Mr Sneeze

1 Mr Sneeze met Mr Uppity in his car. "I'm very pleased to see you. I'm stuck in all this snow!" said Mr Uppity. They began to dig the car out.

2 It was hard work. As they dug, some snow tickled Mr Sneeze's nose and suddenly he gave an enormous sneeze! It was very helpful.

3 Mr Sneeze had sneezed all the snow away from the car! "I'm off to a party at Mr Happy's house," said Mr Uppity. "You can come too."

4 They drove off but they couldn't find Mr Happy's house anywhere. They saw lots of snow, but there were no houses to be seen.

5 Not until Mr Sneeze gave another huge sneeze, that is! It was probably Mr Sneeze's biggest, loudest, most helpful sneeze ever.

6 The sneeze blew the snow right up into the air and far away. There was Mr Happy's house! "Come and join the fun!" said Mr Happy.

LITTLE MISS QUICK
AND HER PUZZLING PICTURE

"Hello, I'm Little Miss Quick. I do things very, very quickly. Take this picture puzzle, for instance. When Mr Bounce told me there were five things different in the bottom picture, I found them in no time at all. Can you?"

Answers on page 63

MR TALL
AND OTHER THINGS THAT GO UP AND UP

"Imagine how Mr Small must feel. Everyone is taller than him, especially me! But some things are even taller than I am. I've put a few of them on this page. And guess what, they're all true – they're not 'tall stories', honestly!"

The Giraffe is the tallest animal on land. It can grow to more than 23 feet tall.

The tallest sandcastle was 20 feet tall.

The tallest dog is the Great Dane. It stands more than 3 feet tall.

The tallest snowman was 76 feet tall.

42

The tallest scarecrow was more than 100 feet tall. I wonder how big the crows were it was meant to scare away?!

Little Miss Sunshine

1 Have you heard about the day that Little Miss Sunshine overslept? I'll tell you. It began like most other days. The birds started singing, but then…

2 …they stopped. Just like that. Their singing hadn't woken Little Miss Sunshine, so they went back to sleep. They'd never done that before!

3 The postman called at Little Miss Sunshine's house. He was usually a happy postman. But not today. Not without the early birds for company.

4 Along came Little Miss Fun. But she wasn't having much fun today. Not without Little Miss Sunshine to play with. "Wake up," she called.

5 "Oh, I must have overslept," yawned Little Miss Sunshine. "I was having the funniest dream," she said, "all the birds were sleeping."

6 "They were!" said Little Miss Fun. "But now you're awake they're singing! And the postman is happy! It's going to be a sunny day after all!"

LITTLE MISS MAGIC AND THE AMAZING WAY HOME

Little Miss Magic makes things happen just like magic. Like when she went for a walk in the park. When it was time for her to go home to Abracadabra Cottage, she just wished she was there…and, hey presto, she was! In the wave of a wand! Now, if you or I had tried to do that, we might not have got very far. We'd have ended up walking to her house, wouldn't we? Which way would you go?

44

Mr Uppity's
PUZZLING PUZZLES

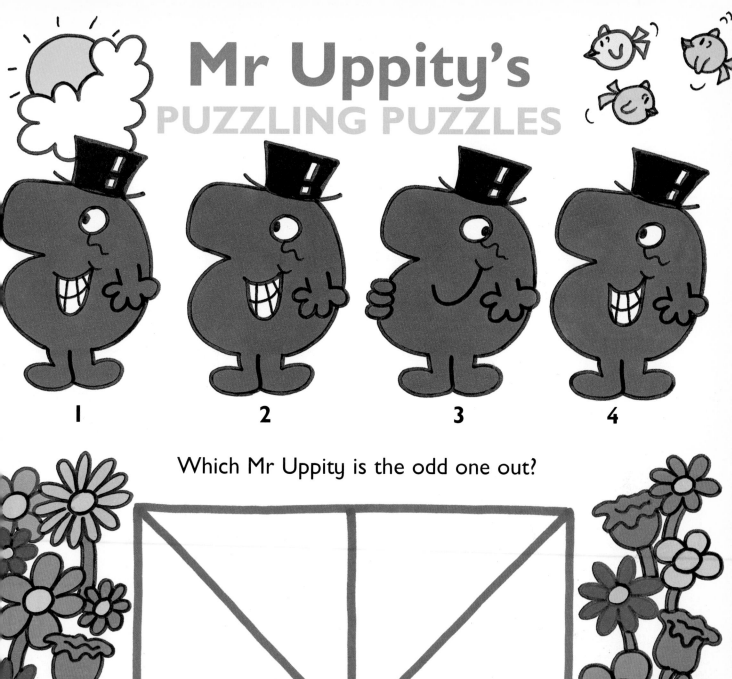

1   2   3   4

Which Mr Uppity is the odd one out?

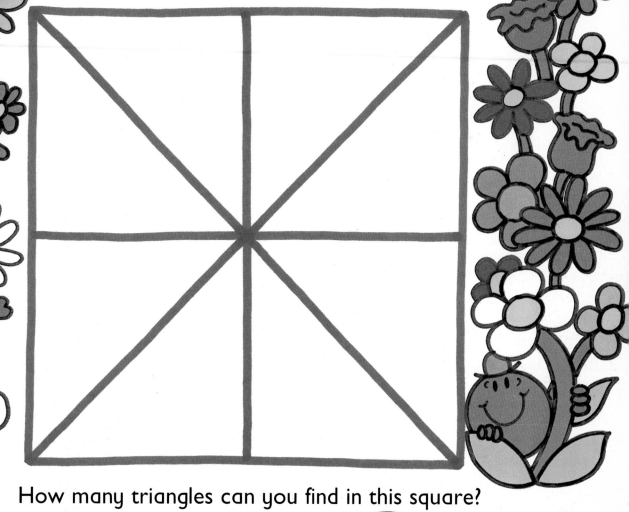

How many triangles can you find in this square?

Answers on page 63

Little Miss Neat

1 Little Miss Neat lived in neat little Twopin Cottage. As neat and tidy as two pins. Not a pin out of place. Except that she had no pins, really.

2 But what she did have were dusters, brushes, mops and tins and bottles and sprays of polish, varnish and wax. One thousand and one, actually.

3 Now, today was VIM day. The Very Important Mug day. It was the day she cleaned the mugs, tidied the cupboards…then put everything back.

4 It happened once a week, as regular as clockwork. As regular as night follows day. Except that today she had run out of washing-up liquid.

5 "Oh, no!" she said. "It's VIM day and now everywhere's a mess. I'll have to buy some washing-up liquid when I go to town."

6 "Until then, I'll pretend VIM stands for Very Important Meal. I'll make a lovely tea, and leave this mess! You won't tell, will you?"

LITTLE MISS GIGGLES
AND THE SHEEP

Little Miss Giggles to Scotland went!
And guess what she did see?
She saw a sheep!
The sheep said, "Baa!"
And then jumped
over a tree!

Little Miss Giggles, she laughed and laughed!
And then she looked at me!
"It's a Scottish woolly jumper!"
Said she, to me, with glee!

FIND OUT ABOUT
FIVE FAMOUS FRIENDS

How much do you know about Mr Men?
Here's a simple quiz about five of your famous friends.
Tick the answers you think are the correct ones.

Find out about Mr Grumpy

a. What colour is Mr Grumpy?

Red ☐   Blue ☐   Green ☐

b. What colour is Mr Grumpy's hat?

Pink ☐   Yellow ☐   Green ☐

c. Does Mr Grumpy ever smile?

Yes ☐   No ☐

Colour Mr Grumpy in.

Find out about Mr Quiet

a. Where does Mr Quiet live?

In the middle of a wood ☐

In the middle of a town ☐

b. Where does Mr Quiet like to go?

A football match ☐

The library ☐

c. What is Mr Quiet's favourite sound?

Woof! Woof! ☐

Sssshhhhh! ☐

48

Find out about Mr Worry

a. What does Mr Worry have on his head?

Worry lines ☐   A hat ☐

b. What colour is Mr Worry?

Green ☐   Blue ☐   Red ☐

c. What are Mr Worry's favourite words?

"Oh, dear!" ☐   "I'm not worrying." ☐

Colour Mr Worry in.

Find out about Mr Nonsense

a. Where does Mr Nonsense live?

In a tree ☐   In an ordinary house ☐

b. Where does Mr Nonsense sleep?

In a bed ☐   In a rowing boat ☐

c. What does Mr Nonsense eat?

Porridge ☐   Porridge on toast ☐

Find out about Mr Skinny

a. What colour is Mr Skinny?

Red ☐   Yellow ☐   Green ☐

b. Who is Mr Skinny's opposite?

Mr Silly ☐   Mr Greedy ☐

c. What does Mr Skinny have for breakfast?

One cornflake ☐   Two cornflakes ☐

Colour Mr Skinny in.

49

Answers on page 63

THE JUMBLE SALE

When  said she was going to a jumble sale, some of her best friends said they would come, too. telephoned , but she was busy talking on her . They went to her and knocked on the . Then they went to 's house. They called for , too. Last of all, they went to look for . She was not at home. "She must be hiding," said . There were lots of at the jumble sale. They were trying on old and baggy old "Look!" said . "I've found a ! It will bring me lots of luck." "I've found a ," called out . "Now I can get out of on time! I won't be late again, ever!" "I've found something, too," said . "It's a . It will make me even wiser!" "Have you found anything ?" they asked .

"No, not yet," she said. "Everything's in such a mess! I thought I'd found a , but when I pulled on it, out came a instead! Then I thought I'd found a pair of , only they weren't a pair. There was one blue and one red !"

The Little Misses filled and with all the things they had bought. Then it was time to go. "It's such a shame that didn't come with us, said . I think she would have had lots of fun." "Look over there," said . Did you look on that ? Isn't there a on it?" "Oh, good!" said . "I thought I'd find one if I looked hard enough!"

But it was no ordinary . Who should be hiding inside, but ! "We knew you'd come with us!" they said. They went back to 's . "We've bought so many things, we'll have to have a jumble sale of our own one day!" she said.

Mr Bump

1 One day Mr Bump saw his Mr Men friends out driving their cars. "That looks like fun!" he said. "I think I'll buy a car to drive around in too."

2 "Drive carefully," called the salesman as Mr Bump drove off in his new car. But, oh, no! He bumped his car into a lamp post and dented it.

3 He drove on but he didn't see the hole in the road and – BUMP! – he drove straight into it! "I'll soon reverse out of here," thought Mr Bump.

4 But he reversed straight into Mr Uppity's big shiny car. Mr Uppity was so cross he called a policeman. Mr Bump was very upset and sorry.

5 Mr Bump sold his car and went for a walk instead. He saw a fairground. "This looks like just the thing for me," he said happily.

6 Mr Bump drove a dodgem car around and around. "This is lots of fun!" he said, "I can drive and bump as much as I like now!"

MR CHEERFUL'S
PAGE OF JOKES AND RIDDLES

MR BRAVE
AND THE WINDY WEDNESDAY

Mr Brave will do the bravest of things. Take last Wednesday, for instance. The windiest, wildest, wettest Wednesday anyone could remember. So windy that Mr Brave's hat was blown over the fields. Just to prove how brave he was, he chased after it. Did he find his hat? You'll soon find out when you help Mr Brave go through this maze!

54

MR JELLY'S
JOLLY MARZIPAN FRUITS

My marzipan fruits are jolly good fun to make – and delicious to eat!

You will need...
marzipan
food colouring (red, green, yellow)
paper sweet cases
a nutmeg grater

1 Knead the marzipan until it is soft.

2 Divide the marzipan into 4 pieces.

3 Colour the pieces with a few drops of food colouring:

   1 piece = red
   1 piece = green
   1 piece = yellow and red
        (to make orange)
   1 piece = yellow

4 Break off small balls (about a teaspoonful) of the coloured marzipan and shape into fruits:

   red = strawberries and apples
   green = apples and pears
   orange = oranges
   yellow = bananas and lemons

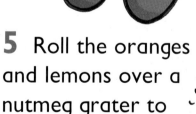

5 Roll the oranges and lemons over a nutmeg grater to give them their dimpled 'skins'.

6 Put one fruit into each paper case.

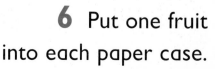

55

A VERY CLEAN HOUSE

Mr Forgetful was cleaning his house. "I can't remember when I last cleaned Forget-me-Not Cottage," he said. "Was it yesterday or last week?" He couldn't remember. "Or was it the day before yesterday?"

Mr Daydream said he would help. But there was a problem. There wasn't a brush for him to use. Guess what he did. He went and asked Mr Mean if he could borrow a brush from him.
Would you have done that?

There was a knock at the door. It was Mr Daydream. "I was having the most incredible daydream. I imagined you were cleaning your house again, from top to bottom, side to side, inside and outside – just like you did yesterday!"

"Oh, so that's when I last cleaned my house. I was beginning to wonder," said Mr Forgetful. "Now I've started, I'll have to finish."

"I never lend my brush to anyone," said Mr Mean, meanly. "Please," said Mr Daydream. "Just this once."
"No," said Mr Mean, using just one little word. He was mean with everything, words included.
"Go on!" tried Mr Daydream. Mr Mean said nothing. He just folded his arms, pressed his lips together, narrowed his eyes and shook his head. Once only. And that was it. He went inside his house and closed the door.

Mr Daydream went back to Mr Forgetful's house. He had gone! Mr Forgetful had tried to make himself a cup of tea. But he had forgotten to put tea leaves into the teapot. He had ended up with a cup of hot water instead.

"Yuck!" he said. "I think something's missing from this cup of tea. What could it be?"

And with that, he went off to the library to look for a book. A book called 'How To Make Tea'. Only when he got there, he couldn't remember what the book was called. "I think I'd better go home," he said.

But when he got back, who should he find inside his house? It was Mr Daydream, of course. And can you guess what he was doing? Mr Forgetful will tell you. "Why are you cleaning my house?" asked Mr Forgetful.

Mr Daydream explained: "…and when I got back, you weren't here, so I picked your brush up and started cleaning, just like I said I was going to."

"Well," said Mr Forgetful, "I don't remember that. But it is good of you. Thank you."

Then guess what he said. "All that cleaning must have made you thirsty," he said to Mr Daydream. "I'll make us a nice pot of tea."

Now, would you drink a cup of tea made by Mr Forgetful? Yuck! Yuck! Yuck!

Mr. Busy & Little Miss Helpful
COMPETITION

To help celebrate 25 years of Mr. Men

WIN MR. MEN CASSETTES
MR. MEN STICKER BOOKS
POP-UP BOOKS
MR. MEN SOFT TOY

1st Prize:
Brand new 14" portable TV and video together with a Mr. Men/Little Miss video cassette

How To Enter

All you have to do is tell us how helpful or busy you have been recently ...... around the house, helping Mum, at school, with a friend – and what you enjoy doing most of all! It is that simple and enjoyable, and there are over 250 prizes to be won too. This entry can be additional to the national Mr.Men/Little Miss Competition that you can find in all good book shops. If you are unable to find one, please let us know.

Write the answer on a postcard or envelope, with your name, age and address.
Send to:
**Mr. Men Annual 1997 Competition,
Marketing Department,
World International Ltd.,
Deanway Technology Centre,
Wilmslow Road, Handforth, Cheshire SK9 3FB**

Closing date 1st February 1997

OVER 250 RUNNERS-UP PRIZES

25 Mr.Men Cassettes
25 Little Miss Cassettes
25 Mr.Men Sticker Books
25 Mr.Men Activity Books
25 Mr.Happy Clocks

25 Mr.Men Soft Toys
25 Mr.Men Book Cases
25 Little Miss Book Cases
25 Mr.Men Pop Up Books
25 Little Miss Pop Up Books

RULES

Employees of World International Ltd. or their respective agents may not enter this competition. The Editor's decision is final and no correspondence will be entered into. A list of winners' names will be available on request and on receipt of SAE after 14th February 1997. The Publishers reserve the right to vary the prizes, subject to availability at the time of judging the competition. Full rules of entry can be obtained from World International Ltd., Deanway Technology Centre, Wilmslow Road, Handforth, Cheshire SK9 3FB.

More Special Offers for Mr.Men and Little Miss Readers

In every Mr. Men and Little Miss book you will find a special token. Collect six tokens and we will send you a gift of your choice.

Choose either a Mr. Men or Little Miss poster, or a Mr. Men or Little Miss double-sided full colour bedroom door hanger.

Send your name and address with your six tokens per gift to **Marketing Dept., MM/LM Gifts,**
World International Ltd.,
Deanway Technology Centre, Wilmslow Road,
Handforth, Cheshire SK9 3FB

Posters:-
Mr. Men Poster
Little Miss Poster

Door Hangers:-
Mr. Nosey/Muddle
Mr. Greedy/Lazy
Mr. Tickle/Grumpy
Mr. Slow/Quiet
Mr. Messy/Noisy
L Miss Fun/Late
L Miss Helpful/Tidy
L Miss Busy/Brainy
L Miss Star/Fun

Collect six of these tokens. You will find one inside every Mr. Men and Little Miss book which has this special offer.

1 TOKEN

Mr.Men and Little Miss Library Presentation Boxes

In response to many thousands of requests for the above, we are delighted to advise that these are now available direct from ourselves, for only £5.49 (inc vat).

The full colour units accommodate each complete library. They have an integral carrying handle and a "push out" bookmark as well as a neat "stay closed fastener". Please do not send cash in the post. Cheques should be made payable to **World International Ltd.**, for the sum of £5.49 (inc p&p) per box. State which presentation box you would like and send to:
Mr. Men Office, World International Ltd.,
Deanway Technology Centre,
Wilmslow Road, Handforth,
Cheshire SK9 3FB

Little Miss Helpful

1 Little Miss Helpful liked helping people. Well, sort of. Like when she helped Mr Grumpy cross the road, and into a puddle. And he **was** grumpy.

2 Or when she told Little Miss Twins one of them had won a prize, but couldn't decide which one it was. So no one won anything. How unhelpful.

3 Today was going to be different, she had decided. She would try her very best to be truly helpful. Yes, really, she would. You'll see.

4 So she went to the shops to buy some tissues for Mr Sneeze. That would be helpful, wouldn't it? She couldn't go wrong, could she? You'll see.

5 She bought some tissues. Extra large size for Mr Sneeze's extra large-sized sneezes. But guess what? She started to sneeze herself!

6 "Oh, dear!" she said. "I must be getting a cold. What a good idea it was to buy these tissues – how very helpful of me!"

MR MUDDLE'S BALLOONS

Mr Muddle has given all his Mr Men friends a balloon to hold. But, oh, dear, look at the strings! He's got them all in a muddle! Can you tell him who is holding each balloon?

61

Answers on page 63